Play on

Sruti Dasgupta

First Published in 2020

BecomeShakespeare.com

One Point Six Technologies Pvt. Ltd.
119-123, 1st floor, Building No. J2, Wadala East,
Wadala Truck Terminal, Mumbai, Maharashtra 400037, India
T: +91 8080226699

Copyright © 2020, Sruti Dasgupta

All rights reserved. Any unauthorized reprint or use
of this material is prohibited. No part of this book
may be reproduced or transmitted in any form or
by any means, electronic or mechanical, including
photocopying, recording, or by any information storage and
retrieval system without express written permission from the
author/publisher.

Please do not participate in or encourage piracy of
copyrighted materials in violation of the author's rights.
Purchase only authorized editions.

©

ISBN - 978-93-89759-61-7

About the Author

Sruti is an Operations & Analytics professional. She has worked in leading Corporates like Godrej, Frost & Sullivan, DOW Chemicals & is currently with the Mahindra Group. Also in Retail & Pharma Startups. She holds a BTech Degree from Mumbai University & a PG Degree from MICA. She is on the Advisory Panel of the Harvard Business Review where she provides timely inputs for the development & planning of its Business content. She has been inclined towards Sports since childhood having represented Bahrain numerous times at the Gulf Zonal Events held within Gulf countries in Dubai. She is also a regular Contributor to SportsKeeda, and the Times Of India, India's foremost Sports go to place. Having run various marathons across locations, She is taking up the Triathlon selections and aspires to complete an IronMan soon.Play On is her debut book and she aims at inspiring the middle class Indian households to take up sports as not only a lifestyle but also as a Full Time career choice and urges them to look beyond Academics. She lives in Mumbai with her family.

Contents

Chapter One: Game on, Girl.   7

Chapter Two: The Game is afoot!   15

Chapter Three: The Games People Play   22

Chapter Four: Game for Life!   31

Chapter Five: The Heroes   36

Chapter Six: Plan Ahead   43

Chapter Seven: Why Not Ironman?   49

Chapter Eight: India, India!   54

Chapter Nine: Move!   59

"One of the luckiest things that
can happen to you in life is,

I think, to have a happy childhood"

-Agatha Christie

Chapter One

Game on, Girl.

I was one of those lucky children to be blessed with a great childhood.

Studying at the prestigious Bombay Scottish School and living in a well-to-do neighborhood in Powai. A childhood filled with every opportunity that I could ever dream about. Abundance everywhere.

My neighborhood, despite being a secluded one, contained numerous residential societies and of course, our school. So, our entire lives revolved around this neighborhood. Bombay Scottish, a renowned school in the whole of Mumbai had a lot at stake, when it came to interschool competitions like quizzes, sports or even the ICSE exams in the Mumbai zone. Thus, we were always under pressure to 'perform well', keeping up the school reputation in all of these. There were tough times; defined not just by the immense struggle or the daily hustle we were subjected to but also by the dreams of guts and glory.

Amidst all this, I was still a shy child. Constantly bullied and lacking focus in my studies, due to which I was chided daily by my stern father. This did affect my confidence to a large extent as well. My father hails from Calcutta and like every self-respecting Bengali, he loved football and cricket like a religion. I followed suit in his footsteps and very soon, there weren't any nuances left in either football or cricket that I didn't know about. I followed the stars – the footballers and the cricketers, ardently debating about each of their performances or lack thereof. Game statistics and game plans were the stuff that my dreams were crammed up with then. I could truly understand the emotional upheavals and the stress levels during the World Cup matches. The India-Pakistan matches were the Mecca for us devotees and I wouldn't miss a chance to watch them, starry eyed and ecstatic every time we won those hard fought matches. I would even judge my friends to be "not cool" if they weren't interested in such games.

However, for my dad non-performance in studies, was an unforgivable sin. No excuse was acceptable whatsoever. To my dismay, I soon realized that there weren't many girls interested in sports in my neighborhood or school and thus, I didn't have many friends with whom I could discuss my passion. And at that time, I truly couldn't understand why it was so.

Very soon, I started finding out about others in the

sports arena in my school who were making a name for themselves in different sports. Renowned in the small circles of our neighboring schools because we all had one common playground. I admired these guys and also the rare few girls who excelled in these sports, along with the track and field events. But all of this took me further away from studies. Little did I care. My energy was spent in making sure I made the right groups of people based on their sports participation. I even started taking part in the local cricket tournaments, initially just as a scorekeeper. I took to cycling as well. At the ripe old age of nine years, how else was I supposed to channelize my energy.?

Too young to understand the extent of the pariah-hood that girls were subjected to in the field of sports, I kept my dreams alive. Very soon I met Nandini, who became my games partner. She was a year senior to me in school and also very active in sports. To my luck, I found out that she also lived in the same building. Initially I was in awe of her. But slowly, she began teaching me her styles and very soon, we were practicing our runs at 7am before school. I would gladly follow Nandini the boss anywhere. She also introduced me to the senior boy's cricket team and we would all play together during the summer holidays. Initially, I was almost always in awe of the fact that I was really in the team. I used to try to imitate my favorite bowlers from the national team. So, one day I would do an Anil Kumble top-spin and the next day, I would do a flying Jhonty Rhodes run-out. I kept thinking of myself as just an underdog those days.

Soon, Nandini and I began playing badminton in the local clubhouse. She was an excellent player and soon she was allowed to play with the more seasoned players on the court, who probably played to eliminate their frustration at work and home., I on the other hand, became good friends with the youngsters of my colony who played on the courts. Very soon, I myself was getting the hang of badminton; the techniques, the subtlety, the slices, the drop shots, all of it. In the meantime, my father got transferred to Bahrain. With a very heavy heart but fond memories, we moved on. I promised all my friends that I would keep in touch through letters (which I did!). In Bahrain, the ambience, the surroundings, the people - Everything was completely new, and I felt a bit weird in the beginning. For starters, I realized that the school wasn't competitive at all; compared to back home in India.

But was it really an unfortunate event?

And Sports? Only meant for those few privileged Arabs who loved it and also a handful of boys who held past records in the school. Bahraini locals held a very high number of such sports records and were extremely fast in Track and Field events. They had even represented their country in the Gulf Zonals & even the Asian Games. The facilities available were world-class. I decided to take part in the Track and Field heats in school, flush with the memories of my past achievements in Mumbai; only to learn that I didn't have any competitor and hence the event was cancelled. This was horrible and I wasn't ready to accept it. Since I was never a class-topper when it came to academics, I needed to channelize my energy and excitement into sports. But the system here wasn't very encouraging. I even wondered if the girls secretly wished to participate but weren't allowed to? Or were they simply shy? badminton facilities in the school premises and this was a huge relief. A lifesaver, in fact. I began playing table tennis with a few seniors and badminton became my life again. It was just like back home. Every recess break was badminton time. Soon enough, we formed a team. There were a few good players in the team as well. Many of whom used to practice regularly in the Bahrain Keralaya Samajham (BKS) and the famous Indian Club. Unfortunately, I wasn't allowed to join the Indian Club because my dad thought that would be a waste of time, taking my focus away from studies. We were lucky though, because our badminton team even had a coach, Junith sir who had played with Prakash Padukone Sir and taken part in the Indian State.

Levels prior to coming to Bahrain.

I made friends with all the boys, so I could participate in the games as they played in the Interschool Sports events as well. I always went to the Bahrain National

Stadium to cheer for the home team and yes, developed few favorites. Soon I spotted the amazing TableTennis and Badminton teams.

We formed a U-19 team and went on to win the Inter School tournament in Bahrain. We kept winning. Soon we had qualified for the Gulf Zonals to be played in Dubai. This was the big league now. A different level altogether.

And this was also the first time when I began to believe in the power of fate. That the Universe really conspires in your favor when you truly start listening to your heart. I got to know that only the men's team would go up to the Indian Nationals. I was disappointed. What about the women's teams? Was there a lack of talent among the girls or was it a case of lack of motivation altogether? Anyhow the Bahrain girls' team was not too strong compared to the Dubai and Muscat U-19 Teams. I was extremely nervous. I had just started to understand that professional sports could take you to places.

Unfortunately, this was also the second time that I noticed or rather was subjected to the whole gender-based discrimination. Junith, our coach was well aware of the level of competition since he himself had played before in such tournaments. However, the proficiency and skill levels of the Dubai and Abu-Dhabi players were different compared to the ones in the qualifiers.

Our strong boys' team went on to win silver in the doubles competition and gold in the singles, thereby qualifying for the Indian Nationals to be held in Chandigarh. We girls had to settle for a silver in the singles competition, where the qualification was through a by.

But then when we returned home triumphant, there was a lot of appreciation and celebration. But only for the boys' team. I was very bitter – because we, the girls' teams weren't even mentioned. And thus, ended our quest for glory in the Bahrain Badminton Competition.

Little did I realize, that all of these experiences were instrumental in developing me into a more patient, stronger adult and all of these would eventually help me in my Corporate roles in life afterwards.

*"Do you know what my favourite part
of the game is?*

The opportunity to play"

Mike Singletary

Chapter Two

The Game is afoot!

Sports kept coming back into my life in some form or the other. And each time it was the only source of happiness for me in an otherwise dreary life amidst caused me to question my decisions in life, specifically about not having seriously pursued sports and having picked Electronics Engineering.

When your heart lies somewhere else and you keep grinding away for long years at something you don't love, it doesn't help anyone in the long run. Little did I know then. Because until now, I had always been exposed to people who had taken up sports as a leisure pursuit.. Although 80% people especially in India focus on education more than anything else, because **'Gyaanam paramam dhyeyam'** (knowledge is the supreme goal) is a litany drummed into us middle class families, from a very early age itself. Education leads to a stable career after all, right? But still there are those rare 20% who follow their hearts. And live their passions. I was about to meet a few sterling brave-hearts who fought hard for their hobbies and stuck to their calling in life.

This, for me was a huge mindset change.

Soon after my Engineering, I joined Godrej Group in the Sourcing Team of the Appliance Division and I was soon engrossed in learning about the technical aspects of home appliances like Refrigerators, Microwaves or AirConditioning units, along with the commercial aspects of running such a business. My tryst with sports was a long forgotten dream and in-fact, hardly ever came to mind now. I was all of twenty-two. That was when I met Debashish, a colleague who was a long-distance runner. He was extremely fit and ran whenever he had time (usually post and prework mostly in the wee hours of the morning or late into the night!) Literally, for hours all he did was just run. I was initially a bit dumbfounded by this amount of passion that he had for running. But I knew that it was something very exciting and I could clearly see the results. Probably I imagined Usain Bolt and so many other athletes, their speed and a huge host of athletic dreams that I saw on television over the years. Soon, I began running as well but sadly, had a horrible time.

I hated it. I just couldn't understand the pleasure these people got out of running. It was causing me immense pain but I persisted, due to two reasons. Firstly, running was helping me attain that athletic look and secondly, it was free.

However, I soon realised that unless my intent was just pure joy in just enjoying the activity, at least initially instead of assigning a goal to it, the pursuit would be a failure in itself. I soon took the plunge into that unknown world of races. There were qualifying races held within departments at Godrej and I participated, only to come in the bottom few. Debashish not only completed his race early, but also ran back to cheer his friends. That was when I realized the amount of preparation running actually required. As is true with anything else! The more herculean the preparation, the easier it looks on the D-Day. Soon I participated in the Standard Chartered Mumbai Marathon for the 21 km run on a Corporate Sponsored team in 2013. I struggled, really hard to complete the race. I didn't know what was going wrong, but with the energy and results the race gave, I knew I had to be there on the road, practicing more. By the next month, I had joined a local running club called the Lokhandwala Running Club (LRC), which still is one of the most active clubs in the city today. My journey with LRC began with meeting Mr. Abhijeet Sethi, a mentor at the club, an amazing runner himself, who later on became a good friend. He guided me well through the Mentorship Challenge Program and a few of us in the same team began running during late evenings around 8-9 pm every day. I realized the stakes were different now and I had to put in a lot more effort from my side. LRC consists of many veteran runners who provide great support to all types of runners, be it just the mid-level beginners or even seasoned runners. They meet at a designated area thrice a week at 6am and are always open to new people. I ran with them on and off for six to eight months, post which I began participating in runs throughout the city and a few in other cities like Bangalore, Kolkata, Delhi, Ooty, even Shillong. I began reading and researching extensively about Long Distance running. While participating in these races, I met many people who ran just for the kick, and also many others who did it full time. I found out that many were also in to full time coaching, having set up their academies. There were people from different walks of life who had crazy Running goals. Some ran Ultra Marathons ranging from 50-200kms and then the king of all Ultra Marathons, Comrades. This is known to be the world's toughest Ultra Marathon of 89kms held in the Kwa Zulu Natal Province of South Africa between the cities of Durban and Pietermaritzburg. It is known to be one of the ultimate tests of human endurance. Here I was, a 23yr old who had just begun her career and was just beginning to understand the hardships of life and these people were travelling to South Africa just for a run? It all seemed crazy in the beginning, but slowly I understood people better, deeply relating to their lives and their stories. What running meant to them. I understood their deepest fears, their meditative state while running, their struggles in other areas of life and how running calmed them. I began also researching about the races themselves. Books like "Dare to Run by Amit Seth", "Born to Run by Christopher McDougall", "Lore of Running by Tim Noakes" opened up my imagination to no limits. However, the reality was very different. I met awesome people and mentors at LRC like Gaurav Bhardwaj - He works at a regular nine-to-five job, but practices 4am early morning runs and completes a 21km or 42km run with ease! There is Nibs who is a seasoned runner and has completed the SCMM Full Marathon 7 times! There were also relatively new runners like Sakshi who despite-being in her 50's, is super strong and has consistently done even a few podium finishes! Thus, I met so many such inspired people from across the globe which not only helped me view life from different perspectives but also humbled and rooted me deeply. It further inspired me to research and improve my knowledge about so many things like, toe-heel ratio, proper footwear, foot types, types of run- wear, our favorite Garmin watches and various other technicalities. This also exposed me to the Triathlon community also known as the Swim- Bike- Run events where the dedication and discipline needed is of a completely different level. But today I know that even if I wake up at 4 am someday, there would always be so many friends awake, preparing for their own 5 or 6am run. I participate in fewer events now, however I'm pretty sure that this community will always be there for me and all you had to do is run. I was being exposed to different facets of life now and it was all very exciting and new.

I wish more youngsters would take running up as a fulltime activity or even as coaching because there are so many youngsters, I've met who are both good and passionate about this. Although the major Metros in India I wish more youngsters would take running up as a fulltime activity or even as coaching because there are so many youngsters, I've met who are both good and passionate about this. Although the major Metros in India have upped participation in this sport not only as a fitness activity but also from the perspective of a lucrative business opportunity, I'm not too sure about how popular it is in the areas beyond the urban belts in India, where although talent is booming, the exposure is minimal.

I know, my journey has just started. In fact, I am sure it is going to be life-long one. I plan to attempt a few local triathlons and higher distance runs by February 2021. My dream is to attempt an Ironman in the next 5 years. The chase is literally never ending. I never want to stop my quest in sports and running is yet another medium for this.

21

"Just Play, Have Fun.

Enjoy the Game"

Michael Jordan

Chapter Three

The Games People Play

My undying love for sports and the thrill and excitement of that competitive spirit that consumed me while playing any kind of sport, must have broken through the defenses of all the makers in the Universe. And the Universe conspired to make those exact moves by which things fell straight into my lap. By July '17, I was looking out for different career opportunities and by sheer accident or perhaps luck, I decided to give the interview at this firm called the DOW Chemical Company. I got the job and soon enough, I began liking my role and figured there were good opportunities to grow laterally and vertically as well. However, the happiest moment was when i figured how serious DOW was with respect to health and fitness of its employees. The office had a well-equipped gym with a trainer, an awesome open badminton court, table tennis facility, carrom boards. There were teams for Cricket, Marathon and even Football. There was also a lot of focus on motivating the women employees to participate in all of these. I instantly knew that I couldn't have been at a better place. My daily routine, with respect to sports, was being set in place. Come to work at around 9:30 am. After lunch at 2 pm, play Table tennis with the Men's team. Now this was something i really enjoyed as I was relatively good at the game as a child. My energy was being channelized well. I used to play around 4-5 doubles and maybe 3 singles Play On 22 matches. I wished I could play like this the entire day but alas! On certain days, I would enter the gym at around 4:30 pm, do the treadmill and work on strength for about an hour. However, as days went by, I realized there was a lot of the crowd who were flocking to the badminton court. This was super exciting for me! Badminton and I went back a long time.

Every day I would be at the Badminton Court by 4:30-5 pm. Initially the Senior players played till about 6:30 pm. I played with them and got to learn a lot, right from respecting the game to maintaining composure on court. We would play non-stop until 6:30 pm. We would all be high on spirits and energy. Post this, many of the new joinees would come down to play in groups. Sometimes, I stayed back to play with them as well.

Despite the fact that I was still only a few months old in the organization, on the Badminton court I always felt like I had belonged here. It felt like home. I got along pretty well with all the players and we soon became friends. Also, since i was new, playing badminton and other sports helped me network and get to know a lot more people in the Organization unofficially.

DOW also had a very active football team that played every Saturday in a gymkhana in Mulund and later at a turf in Dombivali. In September, a Football tournament was announced in the office and different teams were declared. There were 3 teams from the Head Office in Vikhroli and 2 teams from the plant sites ie, Taloja and Kalwa, with a compulsory participation of girls in each team. Now this was one of those highly anticipated tournaments for which the office folks had been practicing for months. excited about this. It was going to be held at a turf on the terrace of R-City Mall in Vikhroli, about 10 minutes from our office. Before the day of the kickoff, we reached there and the knock-out matches began sharp at 5 pm. The games were intense and a lot of fun to watch. However, I didn't participate in the first few games and sat on the sidelines cheering for my favourite teams. And then came my turn. All the other girls had already taken part. I had chosen to be part of the 'black' team. One of the favourites to win since most of them were on the official DOW team as well. They had also been practicing every weekend. The moment I entered the field, things got a lot scarier. The fact that football is a very physical and also a rough game became very obvious to me. I tried kicking the ball few times, but the fervour and tempo of the game grew really strong. Soon I was just relegated to running around the periphery of the turf along with my team. In the heat of the game, there was this one minute, when the ball was passed to me, standing unmarked. I didn't realize this, but I composed myself and started to run with the ball, trying to tackle past my opponents. But by the time, I lined up to kick the ball, the line-referee blew his whistle and I realized that the ball had gone out of the sideline play. I was disappointed. And soon, I was substituted, watching from the to kick the ball, the line-referee blew his whistle and I realized that the ball had gone out of the sideline play. I was disappointed. And soon, I was substituted, watching from the bench. Our game was against the 'Blue Team' which was also a pretty strong team. However, my team eventually won that game, qualifying for the semis against the White team. The semis also began with that kind of explosive energy. We breezed through pretty easily, to find ourselves pitted against the 'Brown team' who were also the reigning champions. They had played very ferociously throughout the tournament with one of their star attackers being   a leading goal scorer for the tournament. The heated game dragged on to the penalty round. But here, we beat them pretty easily, winning the Championship Trophy for the year 2017. Many senior management members were avid football players and were part of the 'white team'. Even their families had come down to watch the matches. The camaraderie on and off the field was infectious.

Soon by the First week of December, the Table Tennis tournament was announced, scheduled to go on for three days. On day one, it was the Men's tournament followed by Women's on day two and finally, it was going to be the Mixed tournament on day three. On the first day, the games got over by 2 pm. So I got to practice a bit with a few tips on improving my technique. I was super excited about the women's tournament and had heard about this girl from the CSR team who played well. Her work team as well, was supposed to be comprised of all the champions. I directly began with the Quarterfinals, having gotten a walkover against a colleague. My quarterfinal opponent gave me a tough fight and the match went on till the 3rd decider set. I won finally, coming from behind having conceded a 12-5 lead. In the Semifinals, I played against a colleague from the Audit Team and it was a comparatively easier game for me.

But post the game, she told me that my game and service style was very predictable and hence I needed to work on it. Next up was the Finals. My opponent had her entire work team standing behind her to cheer for her, upping her morale. This was when I told myself that I had to win this game, at any cost now. The match began strong with her serving really fast and soon she had taken on a wide lead of 7-0. For a moment, I panicked because I hate losing in something, I'm confident about. But very soon, composing myself I got back into the game. I was soon leading 12-7 and finished the first set at 21-14. After my Quarterfinal game, I knew I didn't want to take this to the 3rd decider set and was determined to win this by the 2nd set. And that was exactly what happened.

I finished the 2nd game with a score of 21-16. I was delighted! Extremely happy and proud to have won the women's singles! I generally don't like playing doubles games in tournaments but perhaps it could help improve my collaboration efforts at work.

Women's Double's were scheduled for the second half of the day but I wasn't particularly interested. However, I formed a team with a colleague from the

Intellectual Property Team who seemed very excited to be participating in the tournament. Her energy was infectious. We went on to win the Bronze Medal in the Women's doubles and also in the Mixed Doubles where I was paired with a close colleague from my own team. But truth be told, I felt I had let down my team in the double's games due to my lack of enthusiasm.

After this was my favorite Badminton Tournament again with the similar format as the Table Tennis Game. I was only competing for the Women's Singles. However, on the first day during the Men's Tournament, I got to watch some really close, nerve-wracking matches. I had volunteered to be the score keeper and this got me super-charged up for the next day. Thus, ended the Games Tournaments for that year. Today, DOW also has a few active marathon groups and I'm sure, they've geared up well for the upcoming Tata Mumbai Marathon in January. Unfortunately, my time with DOW ended too soon. But it was undoubtedly one of the best things that happened to me in the last few years.

Getting back and being appreciated for my games had definitely boosted my morale, something that I had lacked for a while. If a lot more organizations took up sports seriously and held more games at corporate levels, I feel that it would be a lot more motivational for all the employees, not to forget the fun factor as well.

I have a friend Sonia Naidu, who plays with the Amdocs Corporate team. She is an amazing football player right from her childhood days. She usually practiced with the men's teams for the corporate tournaments. However, she doesn't play tournaments much as there is hardly any participation of girls in sports like football. I strongly feel that Sonia should take this up as an initiative to encourage more girls to play sports like football. After having worked in a few organizations so far, I'm sure this would definitely lead to higher levels of energy and motivation, leading to better work ethics and discipline from employees.

"Sport has the power to change the world.

It has the power to inspire, the power to unite
people that little else has.

It is more powerful than governments
in breaking down

racial barriers."

-John Carlin, Playing the Enemy:

Nelson Mandela and the Game that
made a Nation

Chapter Four

Game for Life!

The more I began playing different types of sports, the more I enjoyed it. As a child, there was this constant pressure on me, to take up sports strictly as a hobby and was always asked to focus more on my studies. This continued right until my Engineering degree and today, I am deeply saddened to realize how the Middleclass Urban population in Tier-1,2 cities across the country do not really encourage their children, especially daughters, to pursue sports as a fulltime career. They have to either stop it in entirety or pursue it as a part time endeavor. It reminded me of Shobha De's comment about the Indian athletes before embarking on the 2016 Olympic journey at Rio *"Goal of team India at the Olympics. Rio jao, Selfies Lo, Khaali haat wapas aao. What a waste of money and opportunity"* This was blown massively out of proportion and she was termed "insensitive" by most Indians residing across the globe. While her point was not entirely incorrect, the outpour was seen as she trying to demean the efforts of our athletes.

PT Usha who lost the 400m Hurdles in the 1984 Olympic Games known as the "**Queen of Track & Field**" was the only female athlete to represent India for a very long time in this event. Eventually, she retired due to inappropriate funding and lack of various sponsorship and training facilities. Her vision fueled her and she turned to helping youngsters achieve what she herself couldn't.

She started the **Usha School of Athletics** near Kozhikode. There are so many clubs in Tier-1 cities with world class coaching facilities that is definitely helping many youngsters compete and win at the State and National level. However, they are the privileged ones living in cities and thus, can afford a better life. But even they do not opt for a fulltime career in sports due to various reasons. Not to say that there aren't athletes who have taken up sports as a fulltime career. However, these athletes are mostly in the later stages of their lives or have been inspired personally and have finished their formal education already. Taking into account the population for Tier-3 cities onwards, there are many more aspirants there, who do not have access to quality living or basic education. Very few from the privileged society give up their education completely to pursue a fulltime career in sports.

One of the very few such Institutes is run by Pullela Gopichand in Hyderabad known as Gopichand Badminton Academy. Most of the students here are enrolled on a full- time basis. Which means they are ready to take up sports from a long-term point of view and look up to similar players who have defied the odds and have brought laurels for their country, as role models. This is also due to the exposure that this Academy has received and the marvels that they have produced continuously.

Having delved deeper into this, the Northern part of the country namely - Haryana, NCR and Punjab belt produces way more athletes who go on to represent the country than any other region. I would say, this is related to the deep-rooted beliefs of an individual and his/her community and the core values they believe in. Being brought up in a Tier-1 city and having worked with numerous people from non-Tier-1 cities, one most definitely notice the major difference in their thinking and exposure. While the first type almost always wants a better life and focusses on lifestyle because of what they go through on a daily basis, the second type tends to focus on the will to become somebody and having a purpose in life, above anything else. This is in no way an attempt to bracket or brand the Tier-1 youngsters but is a general observation. Also, the core values they believe in, are vastly different. This can also be related to the emerging number of IAS officers, government job aspiring youngsters, even people wanting to join the Indian National Army from the northern belt as compared to the Tier-1 cities. However, that would be an entirely different debate. Young parents can be coached on this, to an extent. If one's basic needs are taken care of and there are enough facilities to encourage and hone their dreams, then why can't sports be looked upon as full-time career opportunities with endless possibilities?

35

"If I being a mother of two, can win a medal,
so can you all.

Take me as an example and don't give up"

-Mary Kom

Chapter Five

The Heroes

Often youngsters in India are extremely pumped up about playing sports of all kinds. Their school curriculums include all sorts of sports and even if it doesn't, they manage to sneak out some time in the evenings be it indoor or outdoor. But this is taken as mostly recreation or time pass. Especially in cities like Mumbai or Delhi, hardly any ward is encouraged to take sports up on a serious notion leave alone play for the country. Only say 5~10% are in the Urban Upper Middle and Middle Class population and among them also, most play upto the Ranji or the Nationals leaving a handful of them with starry eyes. The concept of feminism in sports is still far away, according to me, let our children think about having a career in it in the first place. Hence I thought about bringing this out and highlighting a few of the rockstars from our country and what we can take back as ordinary humans. I'm also trying my level best to highlight the stars who weren't as underpriviledged and crippled by choice to pursue another path.

I personally know a few budding sports stars who've gone through the similar journey and despite which they've only grown.

-Aditya Jagtap(Squash)

He played Squash at very state level tournaments In school in Mumbai all funded mostly by himself. He had a coach but mostly trained at The Otters Club. However as Play On 34 he progressed further not finding any real support and scope in the country, he was determined to not quit the sport in any manner, went on to enroll himself at the undergraduate program at Cornell University. Here, with the best of facilities and training, he performed to the best of his abilities and began playing for India. He played professionally with a World Ranking of 128.He also began getting sponsored by leading brands like Head SportsWear & Salming Squash. Had his parents not allowed him to pursue his dream and in a way protect it, He would have been unjust to himself.

-Simran Sen(surname changed)-(Tennis)

She began showing early interest in Tennis and as a youngster her parents enrolled her under the topmost coach in Mumbai and elite gyms. They spend huge amounts on her training. Soon as she grew she began winning titles in the State levels and getting offers for sponsorships in advertisement from leading brands like Nike. She also won 2nd position in the Maharashtra team championships which won her contracts with many other sports clubs. However due to lack of many opportunities and a rather bleak future, she got through her college in Atlanta where she gets to practise tennis on the University levels and eventually play again for India.

-Avantika /Aarushi(Muscat)- (Badminton)

They have played with me personally though on a higher ranking and from Muscat in the Gulf Zonals. Aarushi and I also studied in the same Engineering Institute and hence i saw both her and me suffer here in our game due to our lack of training ground and encouragement for the sport in general. The kind of guidance and support we had back in the Gulf drastically reduced. There are upcoming players here like Lakshya Sen but again, his father had been an Indian National Coach for a long time and he himself had been a student in the Prakash Padukone Badminton Academy and hence I'm not too sure about the interference of formal education in his life yet. Besides, he's only 17 years of age and probably that phase shall come.

-Arab Leagues(Football)

Football is one of the oldest sports in the country and however we don't have encouragement for it at all. Yes we do try to qualify for the various league games and World Cups but all in vain. The last time that India qualified was in 1950 but she had to return for not having the adequate footwear. Having lived in Bahrain for close to 10 years, I have seen the amount of participation and tournaments they get to participate in and win as well. They spread of Football in these nations are immense and loved all over. Although these countries are not even as big as most of the towns in India, their love the game is way beyond that. Hence those making or have made an effort to stay and play the game for the nation surely require special mention especially our very own Indian National Football Team and few members like Sunil Chhetri and Baichung Bhutia.

-Running

This being fairly new and extremely widespread in the country with a marathon arranged almost every month and various running clubs and coaches around, I would say that Clubs like the NikeRunningClub (NRC) and Adidas Club are doing great in terms of perks given   to the elite runners or those who are good runners and probably can't afford to keep up with the expenses of the Sport. They do have runners who've quit their jobs(inspite of needing it) and become full time athletes and are extremely loyal to the clubs. These youngsters still find it tough to sustain in the country. There is also Mr. Shah (age :28 years) who after being an elite athlete and facing various hassles in the country with respect to sponsorship and ads, went on to compete multiple Ironman Titles (all self funded). He continues his education in Sports in Switzerland and trains to represent India one day. There are more such passionate runners all around the city.

--Shubhankar Sharma (Golf)

He's the No.1 Golf Player the country has produced winning loads of tournaments and titles both in and out of the country. He was lucky I'd say to be born in a rather priviledged family and trained by his Army Officer dad who surely understood the importance of Sports over the traditional route.

--Saurav Ganguly/Gautam Gambhir(Cricket)

They, inspite of belonging to well to do families with no dearth of opportunities, chose to look inside and fight for their passion instead of going in the traditional routes. They are live examples of what they accomplished in their fields.

Although the scope and reach for these budding sportsmen and probably so many is limitless, their efforts would surely have not been given the recognition if not for their parents first who recognised it, unlike millions of young adults the country has produced who aren't as priviledged enough.

Film Fraternity

The film fraternity has time and again produced excellent movies based on such stalwarts in the Sports

World like Bhaag Milkha Bhaag, Soorma, Chak De India. However I can surely say that a middle class family would enjoy this on a leisurely Sunday lunch with family and appreciate the movie and its idea. However how many of them would think about encouraging their wards about the same is something of a doubt. That is exactly when there's immense fear and it's alright if someone else's ward does it but when it comes to my family and taking the risk, I don't think so.

42

"Always Look Ahead.

A Good Hockey Player plays where the puck is.
A great Hockey player plays where the puck

is going to be.

-Wayne Gretzky

Chapter Six

Plan Ahead

From personal experience speaking to athletes in both India and other countries, I have seen a huge difference in coaching methodologies in various places as compared to India. There is surely lack of funds and infrastructure in the country although having an exodus of talent, eagerness and opportunities within the country. This also varies from sport to sport. For a sport like Wrestling, Tennis, Badminton there is huge scope for India however, for a sport like athletics or shortput or ballet there is hardly anything. Sports like Table Tennis and BasketBall are immensely picking up in the country.

Huge efforts are being made by Mr. Pradyut of the Dribble Academy at Gejha, Noida in training in BasketBall, life skills, personality development and alternate teaching methods. The program uses basketball as a medium to develop, extend and stretch the minds of 400+ underpriviledged kids and gives them a platform to learn and exhibit competence. It has also held various Exchange

Programs with leading academies and universities in the United States. However they do not accommodate children from many other states so far which could be something to look into for other states. Another very interesting enterprise called AntHill Creations which is a incubated social enterprise which makes play accessible to all by building low cost and sustainable playscape. It aims at bringing play into children's lives. There is also the Olympic Gold Quest(OGQ) built at ISB,Hyderabad by Viren Rasquinha who's putting in immense efforts to bring the athletes closer and leave no stone unturned to work towards our Olympic participation. However there is still lots that can be done in the grassroots and city levels with the middle class urban population. I personally know a few startups like Coach Crew who connects world class coaches to students. Marathon running has emerged like a business in the country and hence numerous clubs and organisations have been formed for its promotion however the participation from the country is very less. There are those who represent the country in prestigious runs like the Boston Marathon or the Comrades UltraMarathon but the field isn't streamlined yet.

Proposal

One can keep cribbing about the situation of India in sports and how bleak the future is however, I feel if we do not provide solutions to this massive loss, there isn't really a point in discussing this. I strongly feel there must be a compulsory playground in every 3-4 colonies and an indoor sports facility in the planning phase. This it self gives huge motivation for youngsters to turn up and play. A ground being compulsory for every school as well. Also in cities like Mumbai, due to less space Universities and Colleges don't have much area to play and students suffer. This should definitely be looked upon and it's this period that is extremely crucial in a student's life and they crave playing time.

There are Universities like CEPT in Ahmedabad that specialises in Urban Planning. Perhaps they could include sports facilities in their curriculum as well and who knows then how it could impact a person's life?

Academies like Prakash Padukone Badminton Academy is doing some phenomenal work and producing world class players, other sports lacks such guidance (Except Cricket of Course).

A Country is as rich as it's culture and people. Culture is something that comprises of the Arts, Education and Sports. The Sports field can definitely tell about the rich- ness of the nation. Also, if equipments like Rackets, shoes and various gears could be manufactured in house

.This way, it would both be cheap for the players and allow our technicians to earn and innovate. Even now, we de- pend on brands like NIKE,ADIDAS, PUMA and in house sports brands are next to nil. This is also a huge chance to make efforts towards the Prime Ministers Make In India campaign.

Education

Having done my schooling in both India and abroad I can confidently speak about how less the emphasis of participating in Sports is given in India. While on one hand I was lucky to go to an amazing school (Bombay Scottish School,Powai) where each and every student was encouraged to take part in sports and the sports culture was immense, on the other hand I wasn't very lucky and rather happy to study at a College affiliated to the Mumbai University which had zero sports facilities. I literally felt cheated. (I was initially studying at NIT,Surathkal where again the campus is so huge and the sports facilities is humongous. I quit NITK and returned to study at MU where I hoped to participate in inter and intra university sports leagues but to my utter disappointment). These are small things to think about but when thought in hindsight they are life changing. I agree that Mumbai does not have much space but again something can always be done during the planning phase.

Guidance

There is an endless number of youngsters interested in sports however there aren't any such structured centres or coaches as such. Even if they are available mostly in Tier- 1 cities, they are extremely expensive and one can hardly find a mentor for handholding through day 1. However in such cases, if it could be defined beforehand that the child wants to pursue that particular sport as a career, it gets easier to support. This is exactly where the parent's role is pivotal and in case of lower income families, it is a sure shot NO due to the fear of not having a stable income later. More so, in a middle class family I'm still waiting to see how everyone would be encouraging the child to take this as his/her career. Instead of the Father showing him an example of his later self as a Bill Gates/Sundar Pichai or some other Business leader, he would probably show him a Virat Kohli or a Pullela Gopichand. Although the basic qualities of leadership remain the same but thinking genre wise is as important.

"You don't play Triathlon. You play soccer; it's fun.

You play baseball.

Triathlon is work that can leave you crumpled
in a heap, puking by the roadside.

It's the physical brutality of climbing Mt. Everest
without the great view from the top of the world.

What kind of person keeps coming back
for more of that?

-Chris McCormack

Chapter Seven

Why Not Ironman?

The word "Ironman" in itself wasn't known to most people until few years back when the Sport picked up pace. More so, even now most fitness enthusiasts are not aware. Ironman is a Long Distance Triathlon race organised by World Triathlon Championship (WTC) consisting of a 2.4mile(3.86km) swim, 112mile(180.25km) cycling and a 26.2mile(42.2km) run event. It is considered as one of the most difficult one- day sporting events in the world. It has a limited time of 16-17 hours to complete the race, course dependent. Each individual event has a cut off time and whoever manages to complete the triathlon within the stipulated time is designated an Ironman. The Ironman World Championship has become known for its gruelling length, harsh race conditions and Emmy Award winning TV coverage.

My Journey:

As mentioned in chapter 2, my quest in running and knowledge about triathlons began rather late and just a few years back to be precise. However, I began at the earliest solely due to my interest and love for sports. I read up most of the books that were available in this section precisely," Dare to Run", " The Lore of Running" and closely followed the works, records and lifestyles of the record holders of marathons, triathlons and Ironman Triathletes. I studied various psychology texts to understand how they think, of how deep the intrinsic motivation lies and the sheer minimalism they operate with. I watched numerous documentaries available and spoke to many coaches and triathletes. I gathered that this was a scary feet and one clearly had to take the jump. It took me nearly 2 years to get over the fact about how I could afford this or make time for training or even attempt to complete one. However, I took it step by step. Took the smallest steps by figuring things out about my cycle, various other techniques that could be tried on it and increased the time I devoted to cycling. I had also not entered the pool in a while but was now determined to. I signed up for Swimathons held in Goa and different parts of the country and figured out that swimming in a pool and open water swimming were poles apart. I also approached a coach however to realise that I needed way more practise by myself and a lot more dedication. I was preparing myself very slowly for it. There were times when I was going through the roughest patches with respect to both my personal and professional lives and kept postponing my training. I kept making excuses due to some or the other reason. Although my preparation for it with respect to running, strength, cardio, stretch and cross functional was going strong, partly because I was also used to it, the other aspect ie, swimming and cycling wasn't going too well and I was also getting shaky with being gritty. There were heaps of doubt, negative self talk like " This is probably not for me" and losing confidence in myself. I knew I had overcome the mind gap by thinking about the training, participation and completion of such an event but the other half ie, execution was still left to conquer and I realised that I was getting nothing but desperate for the end now which was hindering my will to train. I have had unfortunate incidents of signing up for events and not turning up as I hadn't trained or was too scared. This is precisely when I realised that I had been making a mountain of a molehill. I was also too stuck on the outcome which got me overwhelmed. Also, I began being too embarrassed to approach my coach now.

I forgot the event for once. I started off simply participating and going really slow. I signed up for the Ironman 70.3 race in 2020 and now I'm going really slow and consistent in my efforts. This entire journey took a lot from me and I'm very sure it would totally be worth it.

Hence my sincere urge to all you folks out there to take this journey and figure out if it's worth it or not, by your-self. These races & events are some that require much more mental strength than physical strength.

Moreso, it requires just a little shift in mindset. In the last few years, these sports have gotten more known in India as compared to its popularity in the United States or Europe. However, any form and speed of growth is always great.

*"He who is not courageous enough to take risks
will accomplish nothing in life"*

-Muhammad Ali

Chapter Eight

India, India!

Years pass by and we hardly get to know what we couldn't do and the lives we couldn't live. The people we couldn't become as a result of different choices that we could earlier make. Not making a name for yourself or for your country is one such huge regret that so many of us including me has, something that consumes you to the fullest. It eats you from within. It is something that you really can't help, but only continue doing the best at what you do, not hoping for the results whatsoever. And admire those blessed few who can represent their country in some sport, be it the smallest tournament in any form.

Shifting the Lens:

My grandmother and father have a huge impact in my life more so from the amount of and type of stories that I've always heard from them. Most of them being from the Indian Freedom struggle and tales from the Hindu scriptures. In fact I still hear these stories and glance through the kind of related television that is tailored to the modern day but with the learnings of the scriptures. I was taught to think in that manner whose significance I hardly under- stood through the years. The biggest learning I took from the warriors is their will and grit to work through what- ever challenge life threw at them, their open mindedness and their undying love for their homeland.

This similar feeling of undying love for one's homeland and the will to serve her is that with which one must work. It's completely an inside game and those who even today go on to make their motherlands proud in any field be it education, business, sports, entertainment or anything else, perform their job, their craft with this unending passion and craftsmanship. They keep chiselling away at it through the years with unending grit and will until the Universe gives them the chance to present it for their country, and then its easy delivery. However the one's who don't and keep dabbling and figuring out things through the years, working from paycheck to paycheck, or those who never explore and give in to the long grind secretly hoping for the light to appear at the end of the tunnel, take years to realise the simple opportunity they lost or some do not even realise that unfortunately. I fall under that category as well. Someone who took years to find out and figure what it is she loves and comes to her effortlessly (in fact from her childhood training), which if she had pursued without listening to what judgements the world around had to say, could have been really good at what she loved. That is exactly the reason why I urge each and everyone especially from a very young age to take up Sports in any form, at any cost involved. That risk taken as a youngster, be it in gathering funds, mentor, coach, facilities, or taking a completely different career track altogether always pays off.

Team India!

Most often than not, the term Team India paints a picture about only the Indian Cricket Team primarily due to its popularity, reach, religion and being close to a household identity especially among the retired population.

However, times are drastically changing and other forms of sports are gaining immense popularity; especially with the advent of leagues that are supported

,sponsored and captained by leading Sportsmen, Film Fraternity and various other Artists.

The Marathon and Triathlon community has also been gaining a huge amount of public eye in the last few years especially with the growing popularity of the Standard Chartered Mumbai Marathon race. Unfortunately, the Ironman race hasn't yet gained as much precedence here. Although there are a few who have lately won this Championship, post the media coverage of Milind Soman(renowed Indian actor & model) winning his individual title, Indians are still reeling under the mindset therapy about their will to even attempt one due to various reasons; Cost and Return On Investment being the Top 2.

Hence, my sincere urge to all you guys, it does not matter which form of sport you pick up, Ironman Triathlon is an

extreme test of your endurance and grit, however any other form of sports as well, will without a doubt take you far ahead in your life. Being a Great Sportsperson is equivalent to being a topper in studies, cracking the toughest exams, cracking job interviews, Its all the same or even more. It's all about being the best at what you pick up and making a living out of it, Do Not Worry about the condition of the society yet, you always have that chance to shape it by yourself.

*"Me thinks that the minute my legs begin to move,
my thoughts begin to flow, as if I had given vent
to the stream at the lower end and consequently
new fountains flowed into it at the upper"*

-Henry David Thoreau

Chapter Nine

Move!

We've all heard a lot about how the lack of moving around has been affecting us thereby causing numerous other forms of inefficiencies. However, a huge population of children, especially in the Urban middle class families more so in the Maharashtra, West Bengal and NCR regions these days, are far away from it. Rapid urbanisation with increasing purchasing power has led to growing demand and most parents go to any lengths to keep their children happy. I have personally met middle class parents who live paycheck to paycheck but can go to any limit to fulfil their wards personal desires of fashion choices, holidays, gadgets many a times ending up in huge amounts of loans. On further questioning and trying to understand their thought process behind this, they stated" Our parents could not afford and hence we lived a life of lack, however if we are able to provide for our children, why not. Also, it's a matter of our prestige." I am not getting to what a child has already lost by not moving /running about and will only emphasize on what he/she can do next to better his/her life.

A child to begin with must always be on the run. Whether it be doing household chores, walking a lot, running about. This is a part of basic education and is an absolute must. It is also something that will equip him to be resilient and adaptable throughout his life.

- To begin with considering the worst case condition wherein a child does not have the luxury to afford a sports equipment, he should definitely begin with running and walking upto a certain age. Sports is definitely a huge booster for anyone, however from my personal experience one must begin with basic football or say cycling as a child. These are sports that along with increasing productivity and team harmony, are at very low costs.

- Incase your health isn't upto the mark for your age, Get a BMI Check done and probably download apps like HealthifyMe, Obino (in case you're a smartphone addict). And use them religiously.

- Incase you aren't a smartphone addict, you're already on the right track. Now, make sure in addition to walking and running, you play some sports; preferably outdoor. Indoor games are not a prohibition but, for an overall experience, outdoor would be better. If you could mix up both indoor and outdoor, nothing like it!

- It is almost a sin to abuse the body and not moving around, more so from a very young age only creates a ripple effect which keeps getting harder with the years.

For those above the age of say 28 or considering the working population as a whole, keeping up with the health bit isn't very easy due to the sedentary lifestyle and induced requirement of a particular lifestyle. However, it isn't impossible. With the growing awareness of being healthy and introduction of various customized programs for this lot, the go – to place has just increased. Also, In India in the last few years, the awareness has shot up and is almost like a business in major cities where you have the option for trial and error packages as well as an option to approach experts who will mentor you particular to your specific niche needs only.

There are a lot of people who, these days are moving away from Tier-1 cities like Mumbai or NewYork to interior locations as well due to the cost as well as the health benefits. People have hugely begun realising that although they would get an increased income and opportunities, gone are those days when opportunities are as much of a concern with respect to the geography. With the inception and growth of markets and internet usage, health & well being is of prime importance and other factors have taken a backseat. Moreso, in Tier-1 cities, due to the huge cost of living, parents who want to enroll their wards in sports, find it difficult due to the sheer affordability, which is comparatively easier in other parts of the Country.

www.ingramcontent.com/pod-product-compliance
Lightning Source LLC
LaVergne TN
LVHW041436170726
843492LV00008B/2641